Oliver's Birthday and the Robin's Nest

MELANIE WEISS

Illustrations by Allen Groner

ROSEHIP PUBLISHING + *Oak Park*

ISBN: 978-0-9886-0987-7

First published by Rosehip Publishing
Cover art by Huzaifa
Title page illustration by J.V., © 2011
Photo by Henry Kranz

Ben, Julia, and David,
I dedicate this book to the many summers
we spent enjoying our nesting robins and
to the natural world that nurtures them
and provides them food, water, and shelter
XO

Dear Lily,

Happy Reading

Melanie Wass

Melanie Weiss

Chapter One

If I could change one thing about me, it wouldn't be my freckles, even though I have a lot of them. It wouldn't be having a bossy older sister, either. If I could change one thing, it would be my birthday.

I have the *worst* possible day to have a birthday. My birthday is July 4th.

My birthday is on the same day that America has *its* birthday, which means there is already a big party going on all over the place. There are parades with bands playing and lots of barbecues with my favorite foods, like hot dogs and ice cream. And *everything* is red, white, and blue.

Best of all, there are amazing fireworks at night. Every Fourth of July, my family and I spread out a picnic blanket at the park down the street from our house, and we sit together, waiting and waiting for the sky to get dark. Then, all of a sudden, a huge *BOOM* lights up the night as colors flash and explode in the sky.

No birthday party could ever be cooler than that.

On July 4, the only people who care I am a year older are my parents and my grandparents.

Everyone else is out wearing the colors of the American flag and waving tiny American flags. They are having so much fun, they forget it's my birthday, too.

When I was little, my parents would try to fool me into thinking July 4 is the *best* day to have a birthday.

My mom would say, "The fireworks are so exciting. I don't get fireworks on my birthday."

And then my dad would chime in, "America is having a big party on your birthday, buddy. We are all celebrating together."

But now that I'm almost eight, I know better. Because America may have a huge party every year, but I sure don't.

So that's what I would change about me, if I had the chance. I would have my birthday on a regular day that is far away from the Fourth of July. Then, my parents would throw me a party, and I wouldn't have to compete with a whole country having its birthday and celebrating a thousand times bigger and louder. It would just be a day all for *me*!

Of course, I *try* to have a great birthday every year. I try really, really hard, because I know how much fun a birthday party is. All year long, I see my friends laughing and having *such* a blast at their own parties.

Every summer, my mom and I send out birthday party invitations for some day on or near July 4th. But it always turns out, whatever date we choose, my friends are away at camp or going on a family vacation or visiting their grandparents.

This year, though, it's going to be different. My mom and dad have planned my birthday party to be two weeks early, and my three best friends, Joe, Julian, and Alex, all promised they could come.

The best part, though, is I got to choose a pirate ship bouncy house for the driveway. It has a black skeleton flag, a slide, and *three* cannons. It'll fit right on the blacktop in front of our garage. And they said we'll get to have it for the whole afternoon.

My dad bought me the *greatest* pirate costume at Party Pizzazz costume shop. It has an eye patch and a pirate's hat and a black vest with a scary skeleton on it. It even comes with a gray plastic sword. When we brought it home, though, my mom said I couldn't have a sword with a pointy tip, so she put the sword high up in the hall closet.

"You could take someone's eye out with that thing," she said, tucking it away behind some boxes.

Dad said he'd talk to her about the sword. A pirate needs a sword. But so far, she hasn't budged.

My mom printed out all the invitations. Then, she burned the edges of the paper, so they looked like an old treasure map.

And she mailed them out three weeks before my party, to make sure a lot of my friends could come.

When my ten-year-old sister, Katie, saw my invitation, she got excited, too. "I'm going to be your first mate and have a stuffed parrot sitting on my shoulder," she said.

I very nicely explained to her that sisters cannot be pirates. Then she ran to Mom and got me in trouble, even though what I said is the truth.

"Oliver. In this house, sisters can be pirates," my mom scolded in her most serious mom voice.

"*Arrgghh*!" I groaned, unleashing my best pirate growl. "Well, I am the only one wearing an eye patch in this family!" I stormed out to make sure my mom knew I was very upset.

After I calmed down, I decided I was not going to let my sister ruin my birthday party.

I'm going to laugh at that stupid stuffed parrot on her shoulder and hopefully poke it with my sword!

Chapter Two

A few nights after mailing out my birthday party invitations, we were sitting outside at the table on the back deck, enjoying chicken spaghetti, two of my favorite foods to eat for dinner.

Our brown shaggy dog, Boomer, was lying on the deck under my feet, snoring. Boomer always sits right under me when we eat. My dad says it's because I drop the most food on the floor. So, sometimes I drop food on purpose, just to make sure Boomer is happy.

My dad and I take a lot of walks around the neighborhood with Boomer. Now that our dog is really old, the walks are not as fun, because Boomer is so slow and he tries to sniff every inch of the green grass.

While we were eating dinner, a bird appeared over our heads, flapping and peeping loudly. It had a black head, a yellow beak, and a bright-orange belly. White feathers sprang out below its tail.

Then the bird flew over to the bushy honeysuckle vine that grows along the wood trellis. The vine trails up the deck wall and then snakes across the wooden beams high over our back stairs. It looks like a shady green archway with little orange honeysuckle flowers poking out.

The robin was perched on one of those beams, partly hidden by the vines on and around the trellis.

"Look," Katie said, pointing to a spot just below the robin's roost. "A bird's nest."

Peeking out from the tangle of green vines was a second bird. This one was sitting proudly and quietly in a brown nest of twisted twigs, straw, and mud.

"Oh, how wonderful," said Dad, as he stood up to look more closely at the nest. We all peered into the green camouflage over the trellis. I could see a gray head with a yellow beak that peeked out at me with two bright, dark eyes. "That is a robin sitting on her eggs to keep them warm and safe," he explained.

"Isn't that sweet," Mom said. "The mommy bird is going to have babies right here in our backyard."

Just then, the brightly colored robin took off again from its high perch and flew just inches over Dad's head, cheeping noisily.

"That must be the daddy robin. He's protecting the nest," said Dad, backing away. "We will have to be careful to stay far from the nest, so we don't scare the birds."

"What would happen if they got scared?" I asked.

"Well, I suppose," said Mom, "they could fly away from the nest. And if they leave the nest, the eggs won't hatch into baby robins."

"*That is not going to happen!*" screeched Katie. "And Boomer..." She looked down at the dog resting near my feet. "You better leave those robins alone, too."

Boomer lifted his head and looked up at the sound of his name. He rose on his front paws, staring at Katie a second, then seemed to lose interest and lie back down lazily on the deck floor.

"Oliver," Mom said, "it could be that the robins would be scared away by your party. We planned to set up the bouncy house right below the deck, on the driveway near the trellis."

"No way are some birds ruining my party!" I said, feeling my face get red and angry. "Can't you just tell them they weren't invited?"

"There is a chance the babies will be born before your party and the robins will fly away," Dad said, adding, "If the robins are still here, though, your mom is right. We will need to move the bouncy house away from the nest."

"But Dad," I said, sharply, "don't you remember? It'll only fit on that big part by the garage." I pointed past the nest to the driveway below.

Mom nodded. "That's true. That is what Dale from Bouncy Houses-R-Us said."

"Let's wait a bit and see," said Dad. "It could be the birds will be long gone before your party."

"Don't worry, Oliver," Katie said. "I am sure the babies will be born soon. That nest is pretty small. I don't think they'll be hanging out there very long."

That night, when I was lying in bed, I started to think about the treasures I could bury in the backyard, to be dug up at my party. Then I stopped thinking about my party and started to think about the robins.

How long would it take for them to fly away for good? What if they didn't want to leave their cozy nest?

With these worries dancing around in my mind, I yawned big and buried my head deeper into my pillow.

Chapter Three

I was fast asleep when I felt someone touch my arm. I squinted my eyes open as my mom rolled up the window shade in my bedroom. The sun poured in, hitting me square in the face.

"Come on, sleepyhead. Up you go," Mom said, ruffling my hair, and then she bolted out, leaving my door ajar.

I inched out of bed and tiptoed over to the window. A fresh June breeze flowed in through the screen as I peeked out at the trellis below.

Yup, I could see the robin's nest from there. And it made me think two different things at the same time.

One was how it was neat the robins chose *our* backyard to build their nest. The other was what bad luck that those robins chose *our* backyard to build their nest.

I definitely didn't want any baby birds to mess up my birthday party, now that I was finally going to have a great one! My heart sank. This could become a *big* problem in my life, and just when things were going my way. I needed to push these worries out of my head.

After breakfast, I walked across the street to see my best friend, Joe, and rang the doorbell.

"Can Joe come over?" I asked his mom when she came to the door.

"He's right here, Oliver. Come on in," she said.

I stepped into the living room, where Joe was playing a video game. He flashed me a big smile, dropped the game control on the couch, and shouted, "Coming!" over his shoulder as he ran to get his sneakers.

A few minutes later, we were playing basketball on my driveway. I dribbled the basketball past Joe's feet and had just launched it at the net when my sister came running out the back door and bounded down the deck stairs. She stopped just inches away from me.

"Oliver, your game is scaring our robin," she said, breathless.

"*Urrgg*!" I grumbled, as my shot circled the rim and tipped the wrong way before bouncing back onto the blacktop.

"What are you talking about?" asked Joe.

"There's some bird's nest on our deck," I explained.

"Oliver! It's not just a bird's nest. It's a mommy robin sitting on her eggs in a nest she built herself! The mommy robin is incubating the eggs," she said proudly.

"Awesome!" said Joe. "Can I see it?"

Katie grabbed him by his wrist with one hand and put a finger to her lips with the other. "*Shhh.* You can look, but you have to be very quiet," she whispered.

She led Joe up the stairs to the back deck as I followed behind them.

She pointed to the robin sitting on the brown nest, which was almost hidden by the greenery along the edge of the deck wall. She directed Joe to look up overhead, where the daddy robin had just returned to his protective perch on the wooden rafters above the nest.

Joe's eyes grew big at the proud robins who stared right at us. "Wow. Cool!" he said.

"*Not* cool!" I hissed. "These stupid birds may mess up my whole birthday party!"

"What? No *way*!"

"*Shhh,*" said Katie as she tugged on Joe's arm and guided us away from the stairs onto a patch of green lawn. "We have to be quiet or the birds could fly away."

"Good," I said. "Then I can have my pirate ship party!"

Suddenly, five big crows flapped their wings in the sky high above our heads before landing on the garage roof with a thump. They were inky black from their sharp claws to their pointy beaks.

"*Caw! Caw!*" they screeched, like they had a plan.

Dad had explained to us about predators that try to eat the tiny blue robins' eggs. There are a lot them. That's why the mommy robin has to guard her eggs so carefully.

We knew the crows wanted to scare the mommy and daddy robins away from the nest, so they could steal and devour their eggs.

"*Yeep*," squealed Daddy Robin, as his beak jutted up in the air toward the sound of the crows.

"*Shoo*!" Katie yelled, wildly waving her hands in the air.

"Yeah, *shoo*!" Joe screamed, as he ran toward the garage.

And away the crows flew. But the largest crow landed on a telephone pole high above the nest.

"*Caw! Caw*!" it shrieked from its perch.

Daddy Robin flapped his wings and opened his beak wide. Out came a high-pitched warning aimed at the big black crow. "*Peek! Tut-tut-tut.*"

"*Go away!*" I yelled, cupping my hands around my mouth to make me sound louder. Katie and Oliver stomped their feet and clapped their hands.

The crow swooped closer to the nest. We became three noisy bodyguards, shouting and jumping up and down.

The crow didn't seem to mind. In fact, he dipped even lower toward the nest.

I held my breath as the crow loomed closer to the mama robin. Then I let out a super-loud, "*BOOOOO!*" toward the sky.

In a flash, the crow changed course and disappeared over the treetops.

"We did it!" Katie said, looking proudly at the mother robin, who still sat, silent, guarding her eggs.

Her dark eyes stared right at the three of us, as if to say, "Thank you."

"Yup," I said. "That'll teach those crows not to mess with us!"

Daddy Robin guarding the eggs

Chapter Four

Day after day, Katie watched over the robin as she sat patiently on the eggs in her nest. Our mom had gotten us a book from the library about American robins. Katie had read it over and over, sharing all the facts as she learned them.

After she finished reading it for the umpteenth time, she asked me, "Did you know the mommy robin is sitting on three or four eggs and that is called a clutch?"

She opened a page of the book to show me a tangled nest of twigs and grass. Inside it were four tiny, sky-blue eggs. "Also, a mommy robin can have two or even *three* sets of baby robins every year!"

She began putting little pieces of fruit in the grass near our trellis. And when it hadn't rained in three days, she left the robins a bowl of water under their nest.

I told her she had gone robin crazy.

One morning, after I woke up, I checked on the nest outside my window and saw *wiggling bodies* in the nest, but no mommy robin. Then I looked closer. There were three little beaks sticking out of the brown nest!

I stuck my head out my bedroom door and yelled down the hallway. "Katie, come look. The eggs hatched. The bird had its babies."

She came zooming into the room and pressed her face up against the window screen. After a few minutes, she said, "Oliver, the bird is called a robin, and she is a girl, not an *it*."

"Well, the babies are cute. I gotta admit," I said as I smushed my face against the window screen next to hers.

From my window, we could see right into the nest. Three scrawny baby robins with eyes closed and beaks open to the sky were waiting for their next worm.

"But they have no feathers," I said.

"No. They need to grow those before they can fly," Katie explained.

"Well, they better grown them quick. My party is coming up in thirteen days!" I counted down the days until my party to anyone who would listen.

"Listen." Katie and I pushed our ears close to the window screen and smiled wide. The baby robins were chirping with joy.

"They do make a lot of noise for being so tiny," I said.

Mom poked her head in my room. "Joe and Alex are downstairs for you."

"Mom, there are babies in the nest now," said Katie. "Come and look."

Mom leaned over our heads and peeked out the glass windowpane. "Wow, they sure are tiny," she said. "These babies will need time before they'll be able to fly. I think we should change the bouncy house to a smaller one that fits at the front of the driveway. Don't you?"

"*Mom! No!* They could be far away from our house by the day of my party."

"Let's look at that robin book from the library. It should tell us how long it may be until the birds fly away."

As we talked, a robin swooped into the nest with a worm in its beak then bent down to drop the squirmy thing into an open, squawking mouth. Then it flew away to find more food for the babies.

After Mom and my sister closed the door behind them, I quickly changed into blue shorts and a T-shirt and bounded down the stairs to see my friends.

"Let's play basketball," said Alex.

"Well. We can't right now," I said.

Alex stopped dribbling his ball on the front step. "Why not?"

"Oh, he doesn't want to bug the robin," Joe said.

"You mean a *bird*?" asked Alex.

"Yeah. There's a bird's nest on our deck, and the mommy just had three babies. They have to stay in the nest until they can fly away. Maybe we could play soccer in the front yard?"

"Sure," said Alex.

"That's okay." Then Joe asked, "Will the birds be gone by your party?"

"Well, I think so." I picked up my soccer ball and sneakers from the hall closet. "At least I hope so."

Chapter Five

I spent the whole day and every day after that playing with my friends outside. At bedtime, I could barely keep my eyes open to brush my teeth and change into my pajamas. As soon as my head hit the pillow, I fell fast asleep.

One night, a loud boom echoed outside, startling me awake. Then I heard rain pounding on the roof, followed by another booming clap and a crackle of lightning. I jumped out of bed, ran over to my window, and lifted the blind.

The rain was beating powerfully against the glass. The force of the storm was frightening. I stuck my nose against the pane to see if the robins were okay, but I couldn't see anything through the pitch black of night.

I fell back into bed, worrying about the robins. The rain pounded down from above with a loud steady rush. When it finally slowed down to a steady pitter-patter, pitter-patter, I drifted back to sleep.

I half-opened my eyes again when the early morning sun flooded my room. I'd left the blinds open after checking on the robins during the storm. Groggily, I turned onto my stomach and tried to sleep until lunchtime.

Then I remembered last night's storm and jumped out of bed to see how the birds were doing after that scary rain.

Because of all the raindrops on the windows, I couldn't see the nest clearly. I had to know if the robins were okay.

I ran downstairs and outside to the back deck. Pulling over one of the chairs from the table on our deck, I stepped up carefully to peer into the nest.

"*Phew!*" I saw three tiny beaks peeking out like normal. But now, the young robins were covered in soft, downy feathers. They stretched their necks upward as they screeched for food.

"Oliver, you're up early this morning," my dad said as he stepped outside to help me get down from the chair. "And chairs are *not* ladders."

"I know. But I had to see if the robins were all right."

"Yes, that was quite a storm last night. Well, did they weather it okay?"

"I think so. The babies are all in the nest," I said. "I don't see the mommy or the daddy robin, though."

We went into the house, and Dad poured me a bowl of cereal with milk and a glass of orange juice. He sat with me at the kitchen table and read the newspaper while I ate my breakfast.

As I ate, I stared out past the sliding glass door, hoping to see the mommy or daddy robin appear. Just as I was slurping up the last of the milk in my bowl, the mommy robin flew onto the nest with a worm in her mouth.

"Oh, good," I said. "The robin is back."

Dad glanced over his shoulder at the nest. "Yes," he said quietly and returned to his paper.

"Dad," I said with a sigh, "I think we should call the bouncy house people. I don't know if the birds will be gone by my birthday party. I still want a pirate ship, but I guess it's okay if it has to be smaller."

Just then, Mom walked into the kitchen. "Oliver, I looked it up in the book. The birds will fly away from the nest about two weeks after they're born. I think we need to make a Plan B for your party next Saturday."

"I know!" I agreed glumly, adding under my breath, "I never get to have a regular birthday party."

Oliver's Birthday

Chapter Six

I woke late the next morning, happy to have these summer days to sleep in and hang out with my friends. I dragged myself out of bed and slowly got dressed. As I headed down the stairs to the kitchen, I smelled something sweet *and* buttery.

"Wow, Mom," I said, stepping into the kitchen. "What smells amazing?"

She was flipping a round pancake onto a plate already stacked high with them. When I sat down at the kitchen table, Mom gave me three pancakes and a glass bottle of maple syrup.

"Thanks, Mom." I drizzled the golden syrup all over my plate.

"Oliver, I spoke to the bouncy house people," she said, sitting across from me. "I have good news and bad news."

I looked up, my mouth stuffed with pancakes, and nodded silently for her to go on.

"Well, the good news is they have another bouncy house that will fit in the front of the driveway." She paused. "But it is smaller. And, well, not a pirate ship."

My eyes started to tear.

She moved her chair close to me and put her arm around my shoulder. "They said, since the bouncy house is smaller and we already paid for the big one, they can send a clown along, too, who'll make balloon animals during your party. So that's pretty great, isn't it?"

Just then, my sister walked into the room. "Oliver, what's the matter?"

"He just found out the bouncy house they're bringing for the front of the driveway can't be a pirate ship."

"Oh." Katie studied me as tears dripped onto my plate.

"I'm not hungry anymore." I pushed back from the table.

"Wait!" Katie said. "I have an idea."

Mom and I looked up at her.

"Well, what is it?" I asked.

"We totally can decorate the bouncy house to *be* a pirate ship. It'll be fun. We have all week to plan it."

"Really? You would do that with me?"

"Sure, Oliver. I know the robins made you change your party. And I really like having them here. But I want you to have a fun party on Saturday."

"Okay," I said, pulling my seat back to the table and taking another bite of pancake. "I guess."

"Great," Mom said. "I'll book it now!"

When Katie joined me for the yummy breakfast, I scooted the syrup bottle across the table. "Katie, sometimes it isn't so bad having a big sister."

"Well, thanks." She laughed. "It's always annoying having a little brother, though."

I made a mean face at her.

"Just kidding." She smiled at me so I could see all her teeth.

Over the next couple of days, she and I hung out side by side for hours, staring out the window and watching the robins grow. We were amazed at how feeding the three babies kept both mommy and daddy robin busy from morning to night.

While we sat, Katie told me about some amazing new facts from the robin book.

"Can you believe that each baby robin can eat up to fourteen *feet* of earthworms before it leaves to fly from the nest?" Then she pouted. "Wait, this is so not fair. The mommy makes hundreds of trips back and forth with mud, grass, and twigs. The daddy robin doesn't even help her build it!"

I had a new appreciation now for the mommy robin. But I wouldn't admit that to my sister.

Katie had given the baby robins all names: Arlo, Rosie, and Sunny. I told her that was stupid, because she couldn't tell them apart. She didn't even know if they were boy or girl robins.

Chapter Seven

A few days before my birthday party, my grandparents came to visit from Florida. I was so excited to show them the robin family that had made its home on our deck.

After Grandma and Grandpa arrived, one of the first things Katie and I did was take them around to the trellis and point out the nest.

"We have to be very, very quiet," Katie explained as we stood a few feet away. The brown nest was hard for them to see, nestled in among the leaves. "The babies are sooo tiny."

Grandma nodded at Katie's strong warning. "Of course, dear," she said.

My grandpa just looked at me and winked. He isn't one to make a fuss.

On Friday morning, Grandpa walked into the kitchen wearing tight black shorts and a T-shirt.

"Good morning," he said cheerily. "I am off to pick up breakfast. Don't eat without me!"

Then he pumped some air in my dad's bicycle tires in the garage. Jumping on the bike, Grandpa took off into town. When he came home from the supermarket a half-hour later, his backpack was full of fresh bagels, cream cheese, and lox.

After we all ate our breakfast, he and I sat at the deck table. I made sure we were not too close to the bird family as we played Go Fish. While we picked up a card or said, "Go Fish," because we had no match, the robins flapped back and forth to their nest.

"Those robins sure are good parents," said Grandpa after observing the commotion. "Their babies must be getting pretty roly-poly!"

I laughed. "Yes, Grandpa, they are definitely roly-poly." I liked the sound of that!

"Roly-poly robins," I added. Now I had my own nicknames for them.

Chapter Eight

When I woke up on the morning of my birthday party, the sun was shining in from beneath the bottom blind. I pulled up the shade to peer outside and could see the three feathery robins in their nest, preening their ruffled feathers with their pointy yellow beaks. It had been almost two weeks since the babies were born. They'd grown so big, I didn't know how they still fit in the tiny nest anymore.

"Oliver!" Mom yelled from the bottom of the stairs. "Your bouncy house is here."

I quickly put on my pirate costume and ran downstairs and out the front door with no shoes on. I was so excited. Then I saw it—a boring, blue-and-red bouncy house at the front of the driveway. I couldn't believe it! This was *not* what I wanted. Even worse, my friends were coming over soon, and they expected to see a real pirate ship.

Katie was outside already, in her own black-and-white striped pirate shirt with a red-and-blue stuffed parrot pinned to her shoulder, its yellow beak flopping every which way. She didn't look like any pirate I'd ever seen, that's for sure.

She rummaged through two boxes overflowing with black streamers, white flags on sticks, and even a Halloween skeleton. I helped her separate the mixed-up party decorations, then unroll the streamers and tape up the skeleton. Pretty soon, I had to agree the bouncy house looked great. After all our work, it really did look like a pirate ship!

Soon, my friends started to arrive. Everyone was wearing pirate gear, but I was the only one with an eye patch! Best of all, Blotto the Clown appeared. He made swords out of balloons for me and all my friends. We jumped and jumped and pretended to fire the cannons for a long time. We had *so* much fun, I couldn't stop smiling.

Then we all started some fierce balloon-sword fights before it was time to search for the buried treasures I had hidden in the backyard. Finally, we got to eat pizza and my birthday cake that had two layers of chocolate frosting.

"Hey, everyone," I said after we finished our cake and ice cream. "Do you want to see why we had to make our own pirate ship?" Everybody leapt up—they all wanted to know! "But you have to be very quiet. There is a robin with her babies in a nest in our backyard."

I motioned to my friends to follow me toward the backyard.

Just as we crept closer to the trellis with our balloon swords and pirate hats, my sister shrieked.

"*Shhh*, Katie," I warned. "We don't want to scare the robins away!"

She was pointing toward the deck, where we could clearly see the robins—all *five* robins!—launching themselves into the blue sky.

Mom and Dad came over to stand next to me along with my dog, Boomer, his tail wagging enthusiastically. Then he tilted his head up toward the birds and began to bark. He was excited about the commotion just like us.

Each of the three baby robins tried out their wings and hovered over the deck. Up above them, the mommy and daddy robin flapped their wings and floated slower upward.

"*Bye, roly-poly robins*!" I yelled up to the sky.

"We will miss you!" Katie shouted after me.

Everyone at my party craned their necks to watch the birds fly higher into the blue sky and closer to the white, puffy clouds. Then we all started to wave goodbye and hop up and down on our toes.

My grandparents watched from behind my mom and dad as Katie, me, and my friends all flapped our hands wildly above our heads.

"*Bye, robins,*" we screamed at the top of our lungs. "*Bye-bye!*"

Facts About American Robins

◊ The American robin is a migratory songbird. They usually sing early in the morning and after sunset. Females usually have lighter, duller coloring than the males.

◊ Robins do not hesitate to build their nests close to homes and other areas where humans live, as long as the location provides protection from sun, rain, and wind.

◊ When a female robin chooses a mate, the male may bring some of the mud, grass, and twigs needed for the nest. The female robin builds the cup-shaped nest, lays the eggs, and incubates them.

◊ The eggs are sky-blue, which make them harder for color-blind predators to find.

◊ Female robins sit on their eggs to keep them warm and to help the babies grow. The eggs hatch after twelve to fourteen days.

◊ Baby robins have a hook on their beak called an egg tooth. They use the egg tooth to break through the shell and free themselves from the egg. It can take a baby robin a whole day to work its way out of the egg.

◊ The tiny robins are born blind and with no feathers. They weigh less than a quarter (twenty-five cents!) at birth.

◊ After the babies hatch, both parents stay busy bringing them earthworms, insects, and berries to eat, so they can grow.

◊ The female and male robins take turns guarding the nest to protect the babies from predators, like crows, squirrels, and owls.

◊ Robin, like all songbirds, have eyes on the sides of their heads rather than in front. Each eye operates separately, which is called monocular eyesight.

◊ The wings of baby robins develop quickly, and in just a few weeks, they are able to fly.

◊ When the baby robins fledge (which means, they leave the nest), both parents continue to follow them and feed them. Usually, after a few days, the mommy robin leaves to lay a new clutch of eggs while the daddy robin continues to tend to the babies for a few weeks.

Thank you to my editor, Kathryn Galán, for turning my words and Allen's illustrations into a book we hope is as much fun to read as it was to create.

Melanie Weiss is a writer who lives in Oak Park, Illinois. She has published two Young Adult novels: *Crossing Lines* and *Spoken*, which received a 2019 Readers' Favorite Award for Young Adult—Social Issues. For more information or to connect, visit www.melanie-weiss.com.

Allen Groner, illustrator, lives in the suburbs of Chicago with his wife, two kids and their puppy. His family is his inspiration with their intelligence, creativity, and zest for life.

Made in the USA
Monee, IL
12 April 2022

93816945R00049